Born to be Wild
Little Dogs

Christian Marie

Words that appear in the glossary are printed in **boldface** type the first time they occur in the text.

GARETH STEVENS
GS PUBLISHING
A Member of the WRC Media Family of Companies

Puppies Are All Paws

Wolves are the **ancestors** of all dogs and have passed on many of their features and behaviors to dogs, including strong, muscular bodies that make them able to run and jump. As babies, or puppies, however, dogs can be very clumsy. A puppy's paws and head are big, compared to the rest of its body, and a young dog sometimes trips over its own paws when it walks or runs. A puppy will learn to use its body as it grows older, but, meanwhile, it thinks mostly about playing. A puppy does not like to be left alone because it can become bored or scared. It always wants to be with its brothers and sisters or with people.

The features and behavior of a puppy depend on its **breed**. A golden retriever (*left*), for example, is friendly and loving toward people.

What do you think?

What is a dog's most highly developed sense?

a) touch

b) smell

c) sight

3

> A dog's most highly developed sense is its sense of smell.

Like all **mammals**, dogs have five senses — hearing, sight, smell, taste, and touch. A dog's nose is very sensitive, and its sense of smell is exceptional. Dogs can recognize, or pick out, one particular **scent** from many others mixed together. They can also detect many scents that people cannot smell. Some kinds of dogs, such as bloodhounds, have an especially strong sense of smell. People can use these dogs to search for someone who is missing or even buried in snow.

A dog's nose is always moist. Moisture helps dogs pick up odors. Some dogs can detect smells that are several days old.

A dog's second strongest sense is its hearing. Dogs with ears that stand straight up or can be lifted up can turn their ears in any direction to hear sounds. A dog will learn the sound of its owner's footsteps.

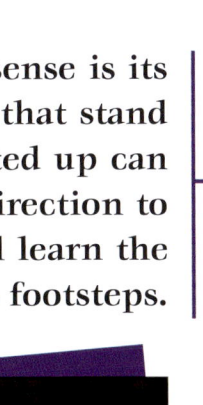

Dogs have good eyesight, but they cannot see colors. They can see objects and animals that are moving more easily than those that are still.

A dog has four toes on each paw. The bottoms of its paws are protected by thick pads that cushion the dog's steps. When dogs run, only their toes touch the ground. Sharp claws on their paws help them grip the ground as they run.

Newborn Pups

A female dog usually gives birth to between three and ten puppies at one time, but some dogs have had up to twenty puppies at one time. The female carries her babies inside her body for about sixty-three days. When she is ready to give birth, she looks for a warm, snug place. After her pups are born, a mother dog licks each one to clean off the filmy, skinlike sac in which the puppy is wrapped at birth.

What do you think?

How many **teats** does a female dog have?

a) ten

b) six

c) eighteen

When puppies are born, their eyes are closed, they cannot hear, and they have no teeth. They cannot go to the bathroom on their own, so their mother licks their tummies to help them.

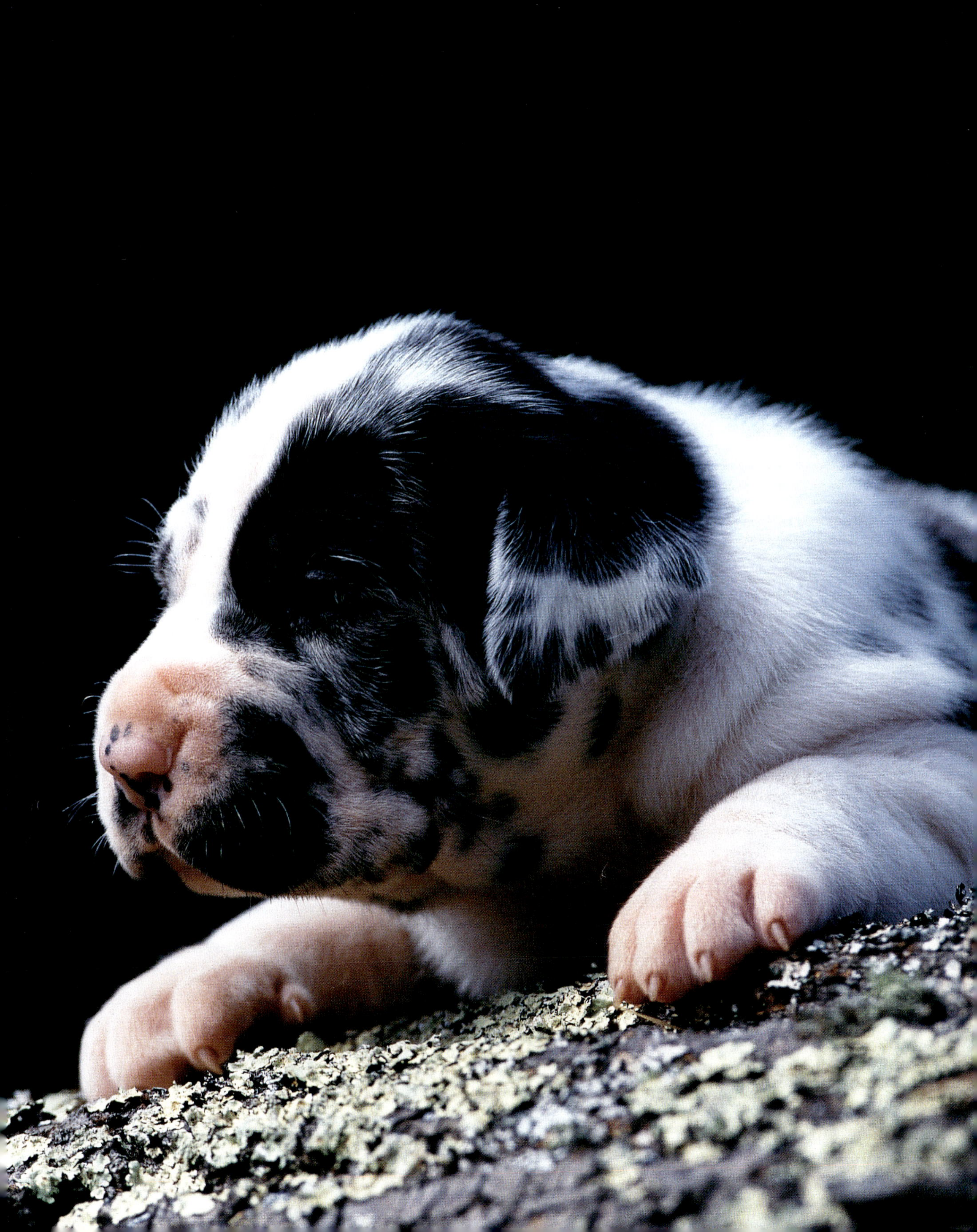

A female dog has ten teats.

Right after it is born, a puppy snuggles next to its mother to drink her milk. A female dog has ten teats, five on each side of her tummy. If she gives birth to more than ten puppies, some of them will have to wait, or fight, for a turn to drink. During the first two weeks after they are born, puppies sleep all day. They wake up only when they are hungry. When they are about three weeks old, they take their first steps and start getting their baby teeth.

At three weeks old, a puppy's first teeth start showing. These baby teeth will fall out when the puppy is three to four months old and will be replaced by forty-two permanent teeth.

A female dog is an attentive mother. She takes good care of her puppies and will even feed puppies that are not hers. Puppies will drink their mothers' milk for about seven weeks.

Little dogs open their eyes when they are about two weeks old. Their eyes are blue, at first, but will change to another color later.

This puppy is playing with its father. When an adult male is with his puppies, he is very patient and joins in their games.

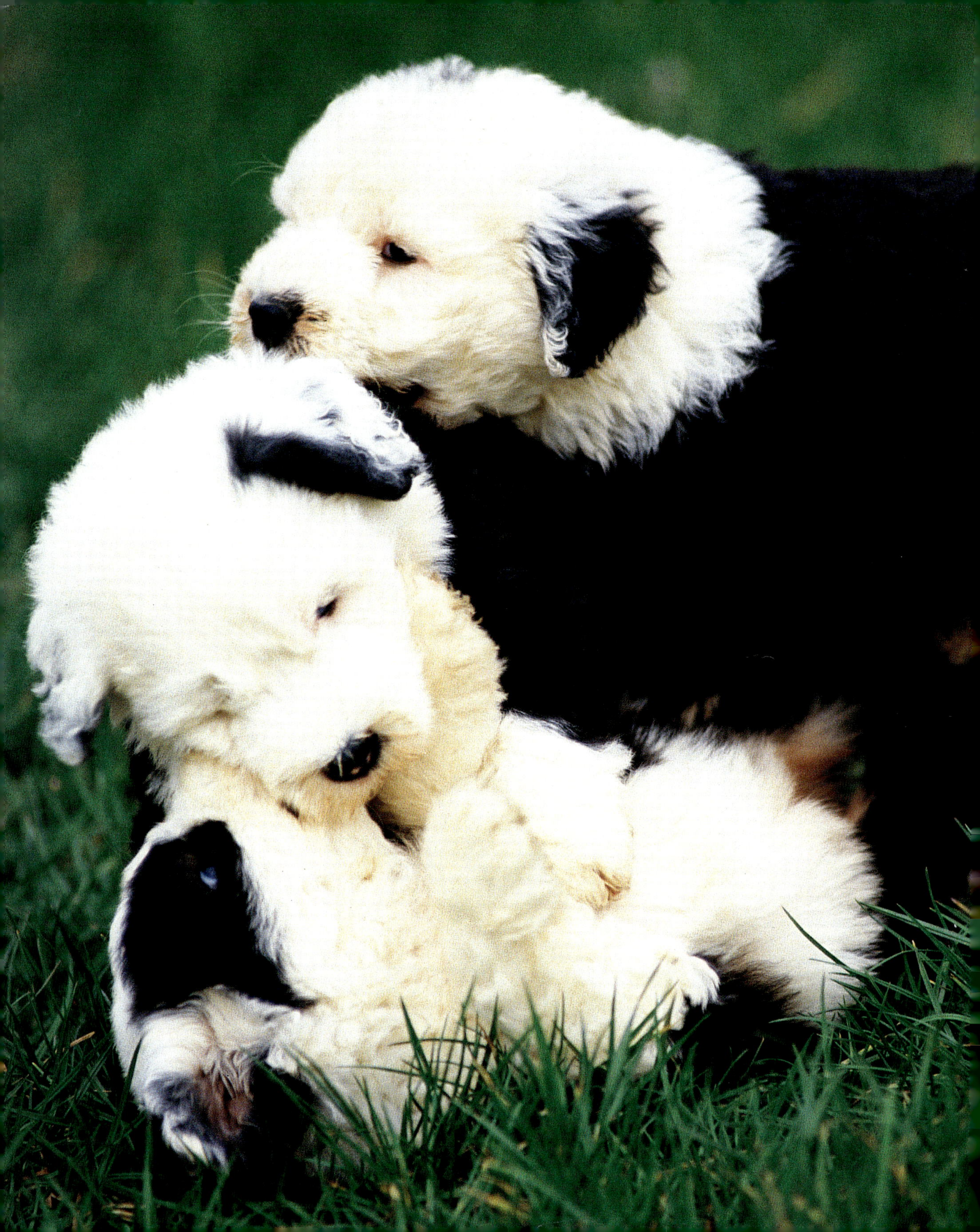

Playful or Naughty?

As young puppies grow, they playfully wrestle and nip at each other. Each pup wants to test its strength and power over its brothers and sisters. Playing together is how puppies find their places in a family or group of dogs. Sometimes, when a puppy wants to become the leader, it growls and shows its teeth. Dogs like living in groups, and they learn very early which dog is the leader and should be obeyed. When a dog is trained well and treated well, it will learn to respect and obey its owner and accept him or her as its new leader.

Playing together helps puppies learn how to communicate with each other. Playing also helps pups discover the world around them.

What do you think?

How do dogs communicate with each other?

a) by looking each other in the eyes

b) by changing the positions of their bodies

c) by making faces

Dogs communicate with each other by changing the positions of their bodies.

Dogs' ancestors, the wolves, live in packs, or groups, of many wolves. In a wolf pack, each animal obeys the strongest male or female wolf. When several dogs live in a group or are together in the same place, they act just like wolves. The weaker dogs obey the strongest dog. All dogs use their bodies to communicate with each other. When two dogs meet, they sniff each other and get to know one another by the way they smell.

When one dog is afraid of another, it lies on its back with its legs in the air as if to say that it knows it is the weaker dog. Lying on its back is the best way for a dog to avoid being attacked by a larger or stronger dog.

When a dog leans forward on its front legs, wags its tail, and barks excitedly, it is showing that it is ready to play.

When a dog lifts its head, pricks up its ears, and stands with one leg up, it is paying attention to a command from its owner and is waiting to find out what it should do next.

When its ears and tail are pointing upward, the hair on its back is raised, and its teeth are showing, a dog is being **aggressive**. Be careful — the dog might bite you!

13

Doggy Behavior

When a dog's wild cousins, such as wolves or coyotes, catch their **prey**, they shake it in every direction to **stun** it. Dogs act this way, too, when they get hold of some objects. A dog will often hold a toy, a newspaper, a rag, or an article of clothing in its mouth and shake it every which way. Adult dogs and puppies have other behaviors that might seem silly, too. When a puppy sees a cat, or a person walking or riding a bicycle, or a postal worker delivering mail, the puppy will usually bark and will sometimes chase the cat or the person. A young pup might also dig holes in the yard to bury bones, or it might lift its leg near a tree even when it does not have to go to the bathroom.

What do you think?

Why do dogs chase cats?

a) because they think chasing cats is fun

b) because they want to make their owners angry

c) because they still have the **instincts** of wolves

Puppies can have more fun playing with objects they find around the house than they do with their own dog toys. Once a dog has something in its mouth, it may not want to let go of the object.

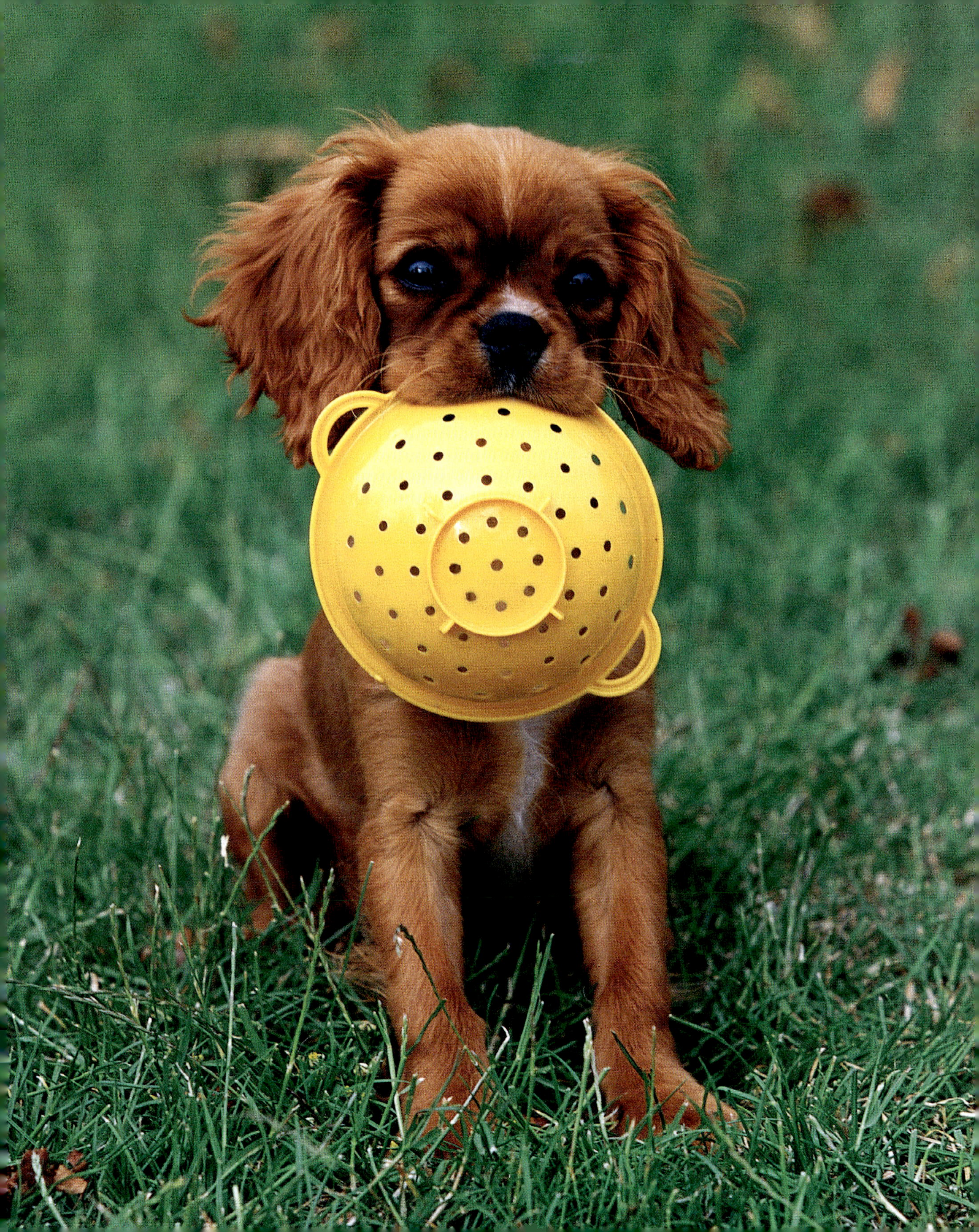

> **Dogs chase cats because they still have the instincts of wolves.**

Dogs live with people as pets, but they still have the instincts and habits of wolves, their wild ancestors. Wolves hunt their prey by chasing them. Dogs do the same thing when they chase cats, bicyclists, walkers, and mail carriers. When cats and people seem to be running away, they are acting like the prey that dogs might hunt. When wolves have too much food, they bury the extra food to keep it for a later time. Dogs do the same thing when they bury bones in the ground. Even though their owners give them food every day, dogs will still try to bury some to eat later.

When a dog locks its jaws together, it can be stronger than a person. If the dog is holding something in its mouth, taking the object away is almost impossible.

Many breeds of dogs, including labradors (*above*), love water. Although some breeds do not like water at all, every dog knows how to swim.

Dogs do not sweat. When a dog is very warm, it sticks out its tongue and breathes heavily and fast. Panting this way helps a dog lower its body temperature.

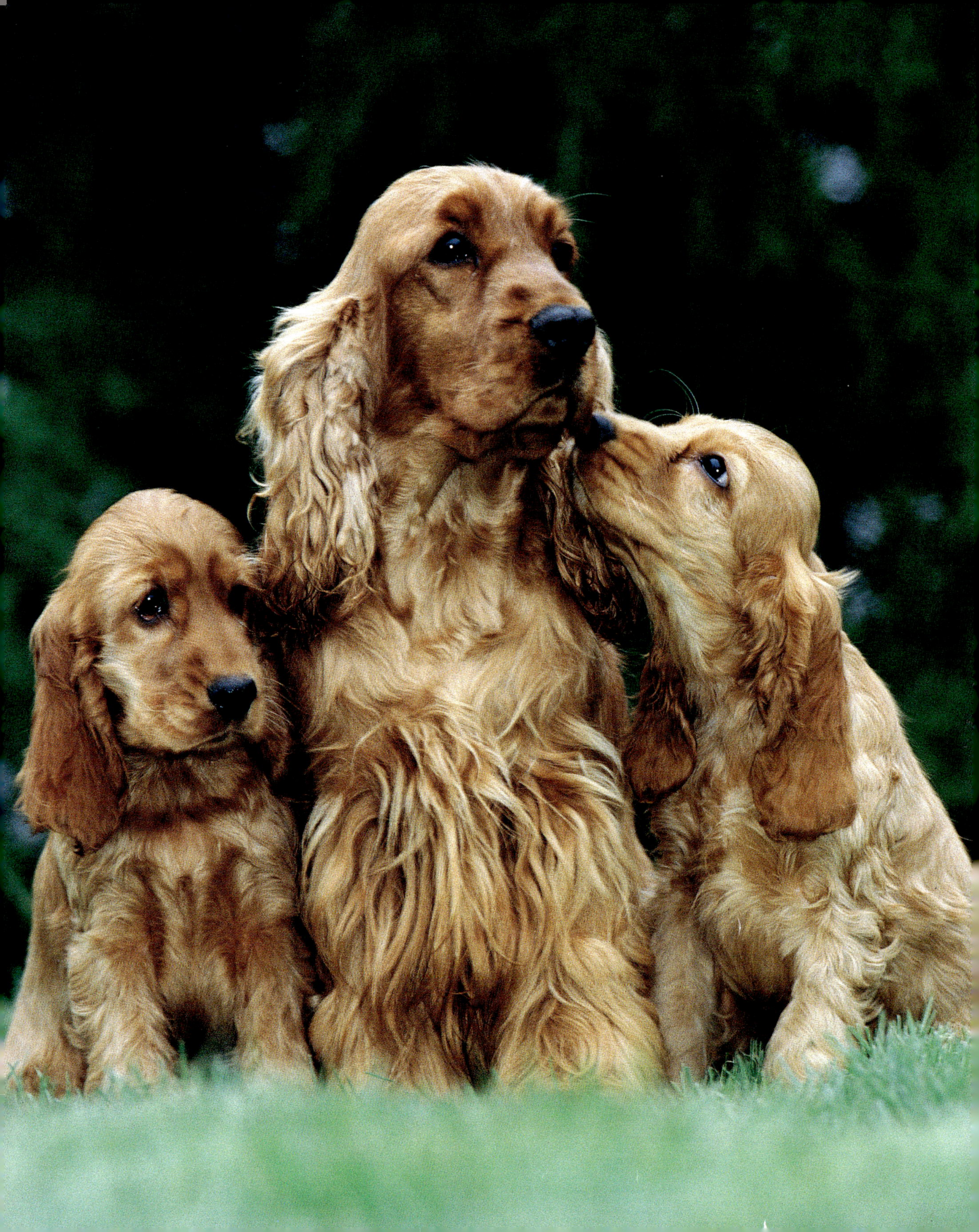

They're All Different!

Some dogs, such as Chihuahuas, are tiny. A Chihuahua weighs only about 2 pounds (57 grams) — just a little more than the weight of three cans of soda pop. Some dogs, such as Irish wolfhounds, are large and strong. An Irish wolfhound can stand over 3 feet (1 meter) tall. Some dogs, such as dalmatians, have short straight hair, while others, such as Irish setters, have long silky hair. More than four hundred different breeds of dogs can be found in the world today, and they all look different.

People create different kinds of dogs through selective breeding. They pick dogs to mate based on the dogs' physical features, abilities, and personalities, then, over time, different breeds of dogs develop.

What do you think?

How can a person tell one breed of dog from another?

a) mostly by physical appearance

b) mostly by personality

c) mostly by the dog's bite

A person can tell one breed of dog from another mostly by physical appearance.

To identify a dog's breed, you need to look at its size, hair, ears, and tail. A dog's ears, for example, can be short and stand straight up, be long and flat and hang down, or even be folded backward. A dog's tail can be thin and bendable, horizontal, bushy, or curled up over the dog's back. Dogs that belong to the same breed will be about the same size and have the same type of hair, ears, and tail.

The body of a komondor is hidden under its long curly hair. Only its shiny black nose sticks out from under its coat. This breed of dog is friendly and very playful.

Bulldogs have short legs and are clumsy. They do not look very friendly, either. But they are also brave and patient dogs that refuse to give up when they are trying to do something.

Dalmatians have black or brown spots on their coats. Dalmatian puppies are born completely white, and their spots start to develop when they are about two weeks old. By the time a puppy is three months old, it has all of its spots.

Yorkshire terriers are small dogs with long, silky hair. They are active and playful, but they are also very sensitive and easily upset.

Dogs are mammals. More than four hundred breeds of dogs live around the world. About one hundred and fifty breeds of dogs are known in the United States. Labrador retrievers are the most popular breed, but dogs that are mixed breeds are more common than **purebred** dogs. **Domesticated** dogs live ten to twenty years. The heaviest dog is an English mastiff, which can weigh between 180 and 220 pounds (80 and 100 kilograms) as an adult.

All dogs are related to wolves and foxes.

Both puppies and adult dogs enjoy being petted, especially on their heads, chests, and backs. Most dogs, however, do not like to have their tails or feet touched.

The number of bones in a dog's tail depends on the dog's breed and the length of its tail.

Greyhounds are the fastest dogs. They can run for short distances at speeds of up to 45 miles (72 kilometers) an hour. Today, people watch greyhounds race against each other.

Dogs have a very sharp sense of hearing. They can hear sounds that are up to five times higher and four times farther away than the sounds humans can hear.

A dog can see things that move better than things that stay still.

Dogs have long, sharp teeth that help them tear and chew meat.

Some dogs, such as collies (*left*), have outer coats of long, rough hairs with thick, soft fur underneath to keep them warm.

GLOSSARY

aggressive — forceful or quick to attack or start a fight

ancestors — groups of animals in the past from which other, more current, groups come

breed — (n) a particular group of animals that all have the same physical features and abilities

domesticated — tamed; not wild

instincts — abilities and behaviors that are natural and do not have to be learned

mammals — warm-blooded animals that have backbones, give birth to live babies, feed their young with milk from the mother's body, and have skin that is covered with hair or fur

mate — (v) to join together to produce young

moist — slightly wet, or damp

prey — animals that are hunted and killed by other animals

purebred — having parents and ancestors of the same breed

scent — a particular smell or odor

selective breeding — mating animals so they produce young that have certain physical features and abilities

stun — shock or make senseless

teats — the parts that stick out on a female animal's body, usually on its belly, through which milk is drawn

---

Please visit our web site at: www.garethstevens.com
For a free color catalog describing Gareth Stevens Publishing's list of high-quality books and multimedia programs, call 1-800-542-2595 (USA) or 1-800-387-3178 (Canada). Gareth Stevens Publishing's fax: (414) 332-3567.

Library of Congress Cataloging-in-Publication Data

Marie, Christian.
 [Petit chien. English]
 Little dogs / Christian Marie. — North American ed.
   p. cm. — (Born to be wild)
 ISBN-13: 978-0-8368-6164-8 (lib. bdg.)
 ISBN-10: 0-8368-6164-7 (lib. bdg.)
 1. Puppies—Juvenile literature. 2. Dogs—Juvenile literature.
I. Title. II. Series.
SF426.5.M2713   2006
636.7'07—dc22   2005053151

This North American edition first published in 2006 by
Gareth Stevens Publishing
A Member of the WRC Media Family of Companies
330 West Olive Street, Suite 100
Milwaukee, Wisconsin 53212 USA

This U.S. edition copyright © 2006 by Gareth Stevens, Inc.
Original edition copyright © 2003 by Mango Jeunesse.

First published in 2003 as *Le petit chien* by Mango Jeunesse, an imprint of Editions Mango, Paris, France. Additional end matter copyright © 2006 by Gareth Stevens, Inc.

Picture Credits (t=top, b=bottom, l=left, r=right)
Bios: Klein/Hubert 9(b); J. L. & F. Ziegler 17(t). Cogis: Vedie 2; Gauzargue 7; Lanceau 8(b), 12, 13(t), 18; Labat 13(bl), 20(bl); Lili 13(br); Français 16, 21(t); Monnier 22(bl). Colibri: G. Fleury 17(b). Jacana: A. Bacchella cover; Ea. Ganes/AGE/Jacana title page, back cover. Sunset: G. Lacz 4, 5(tl), 5(br), 8(t), 9(t), 10, 15, 20(br), 21(b); P. Moulu 5(tr). ©Diane Laska-Swanke 22-23.

English translation: Muriel Castille
Gareth Stevens editor: Barbara Kiely Miller
Gareth Stevens art direction: Tammy West
Gareth Stevens designer: Jenni Gaylord

All rights reserved. No part of this book may be reproduced, stored in a retrieval system, or transmitted in any form or by any means, electronic, mechanical, photocopying, recording, or otherwise, without the prior written permission of the copyright holder.

Printed in the United States of America
2 3 4 5 6 7 8 9 10 09 08 07